Ratsmagic

Wayne Anderson

Story told by Christopher Logue

PANTHEON BOOKS

Text Copyright © 1976 by Jonathan Cape Limited
Illustrations Copyright © 1976 by Wayne Anderson

All rights reserved under International and Pan-American Copyright Conventions.
Published in the United States by Pantheon Books, a division of Random House, Inc., New York.

First Edition
Printed in Italy

(C.I.P. Data located on last page)

Many leagues beyond the ocean where the sun sets
there lies a secret valley known as the Valley of Peace.
"Of Peace," whisper the streams to the leaves.
"Of Peace," the leaves whisper.

Crow believed that the valley was called the Valley of
Peace because there were no humans about.
Mouse believed Crow.
Nobody paid them any attention.

Since spring the valley had been filled with murmurs.
Everyone knew the good news:

"Bluebird is with Egg!"
"Bluebird with Egg?"
said Rabbit. "Then it is bound to
be the most marvelous Egg ever laid."
"We must tell Rat," said Mouse.

"I agree that the Egg will be marvelous," said Rat. "But as Everyone knows that Nobody knows what the Egg contains, there is absolutely no point in talking about It." This said, Rat twiddled his whiskers, picked up his magic walking-stick, and began his daily walk.

"May we join you?" said Rabbit.

"You may," said Rat, "provided you make no mention of It."

By the time they reached Dandelion Wood, Mouse was bursting.

"Do you think it could be—"

"Enough!" said Rat. "I shall take my walk alone."

"Silly Mouse," said Rabbit.

A deep forest covered the mountains surrounding the valley. The Forest of Gloom. Deep in the Forest of Gloom lay a lake. The Lake of Sadness. Deep in the Lake of Sadness dwelt a dragon. The Dragon of Tears. Deepest of all, deep down in the Dragon of Tears, dwelt a witch. Witch Dole.

Witch Dole had a long cold nose and a wrinkled skin; poisonous snakes oozed around her hat; skulls dangled from her ears; and high up on her crooked back sat Scratch, her cat.

"Prepare to fly," said Witch Dole, and mounted her broomstick.
"Why?" said Scratch.
"I want to know the contents of Bluebird's marvelous Egg," said Witch Dole.
Up they flew and down they zoomed!
Witch Dole grabbed Bluebird between her bony thumb and her even bonier forefinger.
Up they flew and away they zoomed!
"Bluebird has been kidnapped!" cried Rabbit. "Witch Dole has her marvelous Egg!"
"Help!" cried Mouse.
And off they rushed to find Rat.

After what seemed to be a month of Sundays, Witch
Dole pointed the head of her broomstick downward.
"What can I do to save my Egg?" cried Bluebird.
Twin beams of light shot up from the silent treetops.

"Perhaps Rat can save us both?" Bluebird thought.
But when she saw that the beams of light came from
the eyes of the Dragon of Tears, and when Witch Dole
steered her broomstick between the Dragon's jaws,
straight past its glinting teeth, Bluebird's heart sank.

No sooner had Witch Dole landed her
broomstick than she shut the door
of her lair, lit her candle, and locked
Bluebird into a wooden cage.
The poisonous snakes on the brim of
her hat stretched toward Bluebird
and flicked their forked tongues.
"This is the end of me," thought Bluebird, "and the end
of my Egg!"
"Hurry up and lay!" cackled Witch Dole, as she eyed
Bluebird over the top of her half-moon spectacles.
"Hurry up and lay!" hissed Scratch, and bared his fangs.
Bluebird guessed that she was safe until her Egg
was laid.
After that . . .
"If only I could not lay," she thought. "But how can a
bird not lay? Rat might know . . ."
But Rat was far away.
"Hurry up and lay!" cackled Witch Dole.

An uneasy silence had fallen over the Valley of Peace.
"How can we help Bluebird?" said Rabbit.
"How?" said Mouse.
And they all sighed.
"Be quiet," said Rat. "I cannot think while you sigh."
After a long time, when everyone was filled to the brim
with an enormous sigh, Rat twiddled his whiskers,
picked up his magic walking-stick, and said,
"Fetch Crow."

"Crow," said Rat, "do you know your way to the edge of
the Forest of Gloom?"
"As well as I know the back of my wings," said Crow.
"Then spread them," said Rat.
Quicker than light Crow spread his wings.
Up climbed Rat, up climbed Rabbit, and up climbed
Mouse.
"Ready?" said Mouse.
"Steady," said Rabbit.
"Go!" said Rat.
And with ten strong wing-sweeps Crow carried them
high above the valley and turned his beak toward the
Forest of Gloom.

"How quiet it is!" said Rat to himself. "Only the swish-
swosh-swish-swosh of Crow's black wings . . ."
"I hope Crow REALLY knows the way," Rabbit
whispered to Mouse.
"Me too," said Mouse.

At that moment Crow dipped
his wings and landed at
the edge of the forest.
No sunlight reached the floor
of the Forest of Gloom. The
leaves were set so close together,
even the forest's edge lay in
perpetual twilight; one step beyond the outermost trees,
all was dark.

"You three wait here," said Rat.
"Are you going into the Forest of Gloom on your own?"
said Rabbit.
"My magic stick will only work when I am alone,"
said Rat
"Goodbye, Rat," said Mouse, and shed a silent tear.

Rat vanished among the trees.

He had taken no more than a single step into the forest
when he saw a cluster of small, bright, hovering lights.
Getting used to the dark, he realized that the lights were
wandering Eyes.
If he moved to the right, so did the Eyes; if he moved to
the left, so did the Eyes; when he hurried, the Eyes
hurried; and when he sat down for a rest, the Eyes
bobbed up and down in the darkness, waiting for him to
move on.
"Um . . ." said Rat.

The forest was as silent as it was dark.
All Rat could hear was his own breath coming and
going, and his own heart thumping.
"A little faster than usual, I must admit," he said, as he
pushed on.
The word "admit" had barely passed his lips when a
shrill, screechy voice destroyed the silence.
"HALT!" it cried.
Rat halted.
Out of the gloom waddled a vast, red-and-golden bird,
with the biggest, sharpest claws he had ever seen.
"I am the dreaded Bombax Bird," it said, and fixed Rat
with a beady eye. "You, Rat, are a trespasser in the
Forest of Gloom. Therefore you must answer my riddle
or become my slave:

> What is thin, but cannot fold,
> And windowless yet filled with Gold."

"An egg," said Rat.
"Pass, Rat!" screeched the Bombax Bird. "But I warn
you – there is more than gold in Bluebird's Egg!"
And the Bombax Bird withdrew into the darkness.

Rat had taken but twenty steps more when,
"WHO GOES THERE?"
cried a voice as loud as thunder.
All Rat could see was a set of razor-sharp teeth.
"Unless you can answer my riddle," the voice said,
"you will die!"
And out of the gloom came the biggest, hairiest creature
Rat had ever seen.
"I am Ticonderoga, Lord of the Forest of Gloom," it
said, "and here is my riddle:

> What is tail, but has no tail,
> And nosing has no nose;
> Is dark as pitch, but bright as hail,
> And feared where're it goes?"

"A snake," said Rat.
"Pass, Rat!" said Ticonderoga. "But I warn you – more
than one snake lives on the brim of Witch Dole's hat."
Rat hurried on toward the Lake of Sadness.

Safe in her lair Witch Dole waited for Bluebird to produce her Egg.

Witch Dole was beside herself with impatience.

"Hurry up and lay!" she cackled.

"Hurry up and lay!" hissed Scratch.

"Poor Egg!" said Bluebird. "Like it or not I shall have to lay you."

And, just as Witch Dole's cuckoo-clock struck twelve, she did.

Quick as a flash Witch Dole pounced on the marvelous Egg.

"Mine!" she cackled. "Mine!"

No sooner was the Egg between her bony fingers than it began to hatch.

When an egg begins to hatch it makes a "crack!" as quiet as a needle entering silk. But Bluebird's marvelous Egg split clean open with a musical "PING!" and, even before the sound drifted away, the two halves of the shell rolled apart and revealed a crowd of tiny, scintillating creatures, clustered about a masked Lady who emitted a golden light.

"Who are you?" screeched Witch Dole.

"I am the Queen of Sunlight," said the Lady, "and these are my subjects!"

Before the words "subjects" had died away, the creatures flew into the air.

"Help me, Scratch!" screamed Witch Dole, snatching at Cobweb, a fairy whose wings were set with the eyes of peacock-feathers.

"I am going to catch each and every one of them."

By now Rat had reached the edge of the Lake of
Sadness.
Grasping his magic stick, he cried:

> "Beneath the lake,
> If there you be,
> Dragon, reveal yourself to me!"

At first the lake remained so still
and so silent that Rat
began to think his stick had failed.

Then the surface of its waters began to ripple, and the
ripples became a wave, and the wave a whirlpool, and
out of the whirlpool came a great scaly Dragon,
shuddering with fury, and pelting drops of water on
every side.
Wings of ivory and horn grew from its shoulders; its
eyes glowed red. Breathing invisible flame, the Dragon
opened its jaws and said,
"You will do for lunch!"
Rat stood firm.
Grasping his stick and looking straight into the Dragon's
mindless eyes, Rat cried:

> "Magic stick! Magic stick!
> Make the lake set fast and thick!
> Freeze the witch, and frost her cat,
> Icify her snaky hat!
> Rescue Bluebird and the fair
> Queen of Sunlight from the lair,
> Waft her subjects through the air
> Bluebird, Queen and Subjects where
> Witch, nor Cat, nor Snake is seen.
> Rescue Bluebird and the Queen!"

Rat did not call upon his stick in vain.
The North Wind came down from the sky and smote
the Lake of Sadness. King Winter rode on the North
Wind's back, and as he swept over the Dragon of
Tears, he waved his iron scepter and cried, "Obey!"
So the Dragon of Tears was changed into a mountain
of clear blue ice.
Deep down in the heart of that icy mountain
Rat beheld Witch Dole and Scratch,
the skulls, and the poisonous
snakes that oozed around
her hat, deep-frozen and still.
And there, too, caught
between Witch Dole's bony,
frozen fingers, was Cobweb.
"Um . . ." said Rat.

As the Queen of Sunlight flew over the Forest of Gloom, the Sun appeared and turned the leaves of the forest to green and gold, and covered its floor with flowers.

So they came out of the forest and into the Valley of Peace.
"Thank goodness that is over," said Bluebird.
"We had better forget it as soon as possible," said Mouse.
Hearing this, Rat reached into his pocket and produced a tiny Witch Dole, complete with hat, sitting in Bluebird's eggshell.
"Just as a reminder," he said.

Library of Congress Cataloging in Publication Data
Logue, Christopher, 1926—Ratsmagic

SUMMARY: The evil witch steals Bluebird for the
contents of the egg she is about to lay.
The animals of the Valley of Peace
count on Rat to save her.

(Fairy tales) I. Anderson, Wayne, II. Title   PZ8.L83Rat   (E)   76-4891
ISBN 0-394-83300-7   ISBN 0-394-93300-1 lib. bdg.